Christmas in Oz

CHRISTMAS IN OZ

By

Robin Hess

Illustrated by
Andrew Hess

Vashon Island, Washington

The Ozmapolitan Press

2012

The ornamental initials at the beginning of each chapter were designed by William D. (Bill) Eubank for The International Wizard of Oz Club, Inc. (www.OzClub.org), and are used by permission of the Club. Bill was a longtime member of the Club, primarily active in the Midwest. He was a renowned puppeteer and designer of puppets, an accomplished stage magician, and a skilled graphic artist with a lifelong passion for Oz.

This 2nd Edition includes several new illustrations and a number of changes and additions to the text.

Robin Hess's *Christmas in Oz* is available from Amazon.com

Robin Hess's *L. Frank Baum and the Perfect Murder* is available from Amazon.com

Self-cataloging Data:
Hess, Robin 1927–.
Christmas in Oz / Hess, Robin
ISBN – See back cover
Originally published: Vashon, WA: Ozmapolitan Press.
I. Title II. Fairy Stories. III. Oz.
813.08766ch

Printed in United States of America
10 9 8 7 6 5 4 3 2 1

This Book is Dedicated to
Rob Roy MacVeigh
One of the most delight-filled persons I have ever known,
Cartoonist, Inspiration, Friend to all,
Finally and forever, home in Oz.

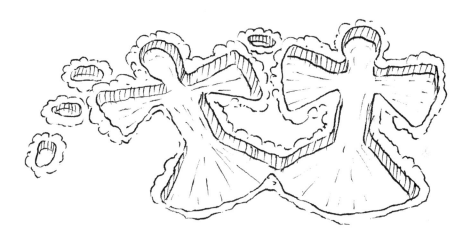

December 10, 2012

To all children, whether they be nine or ninety —

Greetings,

It has been nearly seventeen years since *Christmas in Oz* was first published, but I can still remember the excitement on that third day after Christmas when I answered the telephone and heard the voice on the other end of the line say, "Hello Robin. This is Dorothy Gale and I think you might like to write down this latest adventure in Oz."

Of course I did and I told her so. Then she began to tell me the story that you will read in this book. If you compare this edition to the first edition, you will find some minor changes have been made. This is because after Dorothy read my book, she said, "Wouldn't this sound a little better?" and "Didn't I mention ..." So changes have been made.

You will find here many characters you already know plus a few new ones, good and bad. How would you react to having the name of Merrie Christmas? Let's see how the girl with that name does react. Is Lorabie a Wicked Witch or not? One character you may not connect with Oz, but if you read *The Road to Oz*, you will find that he helped Ozma celebrate her birthday that year. Let me know what you think of this adventure and who you liked best.

Oz Forever,

Robin Hess
27727 94th Ave. SW
Vashon Washington
Hesses2go@hotmail.com

Table of Contents

Chapter 1
Magic In The Mountains

orothy rushed the net, just barely tipping the shuttlecock over it. On the other side, Trot sprang forward, her racket just brushing the feathers of the shuttlecock, but not quite catching it.

"That's the game!" cried Dorothy.

"Oh! If I'd just been able to jump a little farther!" laughed the younger girl. "I could have caught it."

"Guess you need springs in your legs," laughed Dorothy. "Come on. Let's get something cold to drink."

Picking up their rackets and shuttlecocks, the two young girls turned from the front lawn to go inside their home, a huge, magnificent palace studded with many emeralds.

Although these were typical American girls, they

Christmas in Oz

had each found their way to Oz, been made princesses, and now lived in this royal palace with Ozma, the famous ruler of Oz. Dorothy, originally carried to Oz from Kansas by a tornado, accepted Ozma's invitation to stay in Oz when she was eleven, bringing along her Uncle Henry, Aunt Em and her dog, Toto. Several years later, Trot, along with Cap'n Bill, had been swept to Oz by a whirlpool off the coast of California, and they, too, had settled in Oz.

To look at them, you would think that Dorothy was about eleven years old and Trot about ten. Actually, in this marvelous fairyland, anyone can remain the same age for just as long as they might wish. So for nearly 100 years, Dorothy has been perfectly happy as an eleven-year-old, and Trot as a ten-year-old. Both have had much more experience than their youthful looks would indicate.

As they reached the palace steps, the strangest looking man sprang through the front gate. Yes, he sprang! For that was what he was made of — springs. His legs were springs. His arms and fingers were springs. His neck was a spring. His body was one big spring. Even the curly hair on top of his head was made up of tiny springs. Wouldn't such a person be a total amazement to you? I thought so, and certainly, despite all the other strange personages they had met, Trot and Dorothy would have been surprised too, except that they already knew him as the Caretaker of the Viridian Springs,

Magic in the Mountains

source of most of the water for the Emerald City.

"Hurry! Ozma must hear!" he exclaimed. "Most terrible news!"

"Why? What is it?" asked Dorothy.

"Oh!" he exclaimed, bobbing up and down on his springs. "Snow in Oz! On Viridian Mountain. Buildings going up! In the valley beyond. Terrible messages! On rocks in the pass." His words bounced out of him just as he bounced on his springy legs.

Trot looked a little puzzled at his excitement. Dorothy giggled a bit, thinking it sounded more like fun than something terrible, but in serious tones she said, "Come

Christmas in Oz

along. I think I know where to find Ozma," and leading the way went on up the stairs and through the ornate doorways into the Palace.

Just inside the doors a young boy named Button-Bright fell in step with them. Down the hall they went. Turn here. Up the stairs. Down another hall. One more turn, and then Dorothy knocked on a door.

"Who's there?" called a winsome voice from inside.

"It's Dorothy and Trot and Button-Bright with Springer."

With Dorothy's first words, footsteps could be heard inside and soon the door opened upon a lovely room decorated primarily in green. A brocaded couch sat along one wall and several comfortable looking matching chairs were scattered around the room. Great windows, framed in frothy green organdy, looked out on lovely gardens. An ornate desk was at one end of the room and a table with fresh fruits at the other. The door was held open by an older girl in a simple green dress. Her black hair was topped by a remarkably tall and narrow crown and large red poppies framed her fair face. This was the Queen of all Oz, but she greeted them all as friends and then said, "So, Springer, what brings you to the Emerald City?"

"Oh, your majesty! Most awful! Most awful events!" With care, Ozma took his metallic hands in her own as she said, "Here, sit down a bit and take your time telling me what this is all about."

Magic in the Mountains

Once he was seated and had calmed down a bit, Springer was able to talk in normal sentences. He explained how he had noticed a strange whiteness on the top of Viridian Mountain several days ago. So, yesterday morning he had gone up to check on it, and for the first time in his life was confronted with snow! Though he had heard of it before, he had never seen any and knew that in Oz, it always seemed to be a herald of bad things. And this certainly looked bad, for there, on one of the rocks, had been painted:

THIS WILL NEVER BE.
CURSED MAY IT BE,
AND ALL BECAUSE OF ME.
SO SAYS LORABIE!

He saw not only the curse, but snow on all the mountains around the valley beyond Viridian Mountain. And in the middle of the valley, there was a cluster of brand new buildings, buildings like none he had ever seen before. And they had sprung up since his last visit to the valley only two months before. Sneaking around, being careful to keep out of sight of those buildings, he found the same scrawling upon rocks at each pass around the valley.

When he had finished his story, Dorothy asked, "Snow? How could it be there and how could it be cold enough to stay?"

Christmas in Oz

"What 'will never be' and what will be 'cursed?'" wondered Trot.

"And who's Lorabie?" asked Button-Bright.

"Whoever Lorabie is," said Ozma, "it is certainly unlawful for her to be doing any real curses. You did the right thing, Springer. We have to go there and find out what this is all about."

"Oh! Can I go?" cried Trot. "It sounds so exciting!"

"Yes," answered Ozma. "I think it best if we take a large group." Then she walked over to pull her bell cord and continued, saying, I'll have Omby Amby take the word around to everyone. In the meantime, let's start making our plans to leave in the morning."

THIS WILL NEVER BE
CURSED MAY IT BE
AND ALL BECAUSE OF ME
SO SAYS LORABIE

Chapter 2
The Magic Umbrella

ushing her long brown hair back from her face, Chris laid the book on the window seat beside her. Even the cold snow she saw falling in the lamplight could not dissipate the warm feeling she had after reading of Dorothy's adventures.

Ozma, Tik-Tok, the Nome King! Wouldn't it be fun to be like Dorothy and actually travel to Oz? All her life she had known about it, but only from the movie where it was treated like a dream. Only recently had she discovered the books, where Oz was treated like a real-life adventure. She had run into them in her library back home in Olympia, Washington, and she enjoyed reading *The Wizard of Oz* as a book so much that she had checked out the next four Oz books to read on this

Christmas in Oz

Christmas trip to Philadelphia.

Awakening early this morning, Chris had Oz on her mind, so she had come downstairs before anyone else to finish the book she had started the day before. Done with it now, she looked at the old umbrella hanging on the rack by the window. After bringing them in from the airport last night, Uncle Walt had brought out this old umbrella, took it in his hands and asked, "What does this look like to you?"

She had stammered a bit before saying, "Why, old and brown and big and, well, nearly worn-out."

"Yes," laughed Uncle Walt, "old and brown and big, but let's hope it is not worn-out, for this is a magic umbrella – our Good Luck Umbrella! So long as we have it, our fortune is always good."

The whole family was gathered together and Chris's mother had objected, "Oh now, Uncle Walt, you don't believe that old superstition do you?"

"Superstitious, I am not, but you cannot deny that we have always prospered and been happy when this umbrella was in the house. Good fortune has, unmistakably, gone with us wherever we have gone."

Turning to Chris, he continued, "The only real misfortune we ever had was before I was born and my older brother, Saladin, disappeared. And, do you know what?"

Chris had looked at him with her big brown eyes and shook her head.

The Magic Umbrella

Putting all the drama into it that he could, Walt pointed with his forefinger and answered, "That umbrella had disappeared!"

"Saladin was never heard from again, but in a few days the old umbrella mysteriously returned to its regular place up in the attic, and our good fortune returned, uninterrupted, to this very day."

"But you don't keep it in the attic anymore?" asked Chris's father.

"Oh yes, but I brought it down today just so I could explain its magic to you, Chris.

"Now, before any of you object, I want to be sure that Chris understands that this umbrella is only a symbol. The magic, Chris, is in you. Believe that you are going to have bad luck and you will. Believe that you are going to have good luck and you will. No guarantee, but it helps. The umbrella has only encouraged me to always believe that things will work out. Not things like winning at a game of cards. With those I take my chances. But my optimism remains strong in the important things like being my best self."

Just then Aunt Lydia had brought in a try of cookies for everyone and said, "Walter, tell her where it came from."

"Ah yes. Family tradition says it was brought back from Arabia by one of our great-great-and-ever-so-great-grandfathers who was there as a knight in the year 1000 A. D.

Christmas in Oz

"But," said Mr. Pedersen, "I doubt that there would have been any such things as umbrellas back then."

"As a matter of fact," replied Walter, "there were. Once, for the fun of it, I decided to study up on umbrellas and found that they have existed for thousands of years. Europe didn't seem to have them until the Seventeenth Century, but China, Egypt and the Middle East did."

"Humph! And I always supposed it was a fairly new invention," said Chris's dad.

"You can learn the darnedest things with a little study," said Walt. "But, let me see, where was I? Oh, yes.

The Magic Umbrella

Over many generations this umbrella has always been handed down from father to son. But there are no more sons in our family. I have had no children at all, and my only sister had but one child, and that, Chris, was you. Since her only child is you, Chris, instead of going from father to son, this time the umbrella goes from great-uncle to grandniece. I am getting old, and when you go home, I want you to take the umbrella with you."

That had been last night. Now, instead of starting on another book, Chris, curious about the umbrella, took it down to examine it more closely. It was a very big umbrella and had the head of an elephant carved into its handle, two red stones for eyes and a curved trunk as a convenient handle. Holding it and looking at the snow falling and falling, she thought about Oz where it never snows, and the marvelous adventures that other girls had had in Oz and said aloud, "I wish I were in Oz."

No sooner were the words out of her mouth than the umbrella gave a great tug and dragged her straight toward the front door.

"We're going to crash!" she cried out. But just at the last moment the lock on the door went click-click and the door flew open. Out into the cold air of the morning they went. The umbrella opened of its own accord and rapidly pulled her into the snow filled sky.

"I don't think this is very good luck," groaned Chris. "Why didn't I let go before it was too late?"

Now she clung desperately to the umbrella, although

Christmas in Oz

she soon realized that the snow they were flying through was not touching her and what should have been very cold air felt almost warm. On they went, up above the clouds and just as they cleared the tops of them, she momentarily forgot her plight. The glory of seeing the sunrise from so high in the sky overwhelmed any fears she had.

But then Chris began to realize the truth of the situation. She was traveling through the sky, not "as if by magic," but actually *by* magic – the magic of the umbrella!

She mused on that a bit, but then she began to worry again. She was getting farther and farther from home and her parents would be worrying. Then she thought to herself, *How do I give this umbrella directions?* Then, speaking aloud, she said, "Umbrella, please take me home to Philadelphia!"

When it did not turn she thought, *Maybe it just responds to wishes,* then, loudly again, she said, "I wish I were back home in Philadelphia!" Still no turning. She pleaded and she threatened and she tried a couple more wishes, but nothing could make the umbrella swerve.

Just then they began descending through the clouds, and soon, below, her she saw a lovely city with towers and walls gleaming in the bright sunlight. She thought, *How could there be all this sunshine when I just came through heavy clouds?*

She looked up, expecting to see again all those

13

Christmas in Oz

clouds, but the sky was perfectly clear. *Now how can that be?* she thought.

Looking down again, she saw tall spires marking a great building toward which the umbrella seemed to be taking her. Jewels seemed to sparkle from its walls. As they drew closer, she could see quite a large group of people and thought, *Well, well, a welcoming committee. I hope they are friendly.*

As she drew nearer to the people, she realized they were not a welcoming committee, but a group of people and animals getting ready for a trip. There were no cars or bicycles, but there were packs and two horses were preparing to pull an open cart - horses? Not horses. A lion and a tiger! And there's a copper man and a soldier with a long green beard! The Cowardly Lion? The Hungry Tiger? Tik-Tok? The Soldier with Green Whiskers! How could that be? They were all characters from Oz books and were only make believe. But she had wished to go to Oz, and then the umbrella took over and this is the place it had brought her to.

As her feet touched the ground, she found herself right in front of a lovely girl with long black hair, a strangely tall, thin crown on her head and two red poppies in her hair. Still not able to believe who this must be, Chris did what she hoped would pass for a curtsey, just as the girl in front of her said, "My, my, but you pick an unusual way to arrive. Where did you come from?"

For a moment, Chris was speechless. So much had

The Magic Umbrella

happened. Then, remembering her manners, she said, "Oh, excuse me. My name is Chris Pedersen and, although I just came from Philadelphia, I'm actually from Olympia."

With a sweet little laugh, the girl answered "Well then, welcome to Oz. I am Princess Ozma, and you see many of my friends gathered here. I hope they will soon be your friends, too."

Blushing a bit, Chris kind of mumbled, "I'm sure they will be."

About that time, a younger girl, who looked about the same age as Chris and was dressed in a blue gingham dress and white pinafore, came over and said, "My name is Dorothy, and I used to live in Kansas. I'm sure we will be good friends."

Chris's heart almost stopped beating. "You-you're the real Dorothy? My goodness! I can't believe all this."

"We may be hard to believe, but that's quite an umbrella you have yourself," replied Dorothy. "Where did it come from? They didn't use to have magic in America."

"They still don't," replied Chris. "I can't figure out, myself, how this umbrella could carry me here."

Now Trot chimed in, saying, "Cap'n Bill and Button-Bright and I once travelled by umbrella. But that was over a century ago. And Button-Bright lost his umbrella."

"'Lost' is his middle name," giggled Dorothy.

"And that is just what he is again," remarked Ozma.

Christmas in Oz

"He wanted to go with us, but he hasn't shown up yet, so I guess we'll just have to go without him."

"He'll turn up," remarked Trot. "He always does." Then she added, "Maybe his old umbrella has just turned up again, too."

Turning to Chris, Ozma asked, "How would you like to go with us? We have a mystery in the mountains south of here and are setting out on an expedition to determine what's going on." As Chris paused, she added, "I shouldn't think it would be anything dangerous."

"It isn't that. It just seems like Mom and Dad ought to know where I am."

"Indeed. So, we'll just send them a note before we leave."

"But there isn't any mail delivery from Oz to Philadelphia?" said Chris. Then after a slight pause she added, "Is there?"

"Better than that," said Ozma as she touched the big jeweled belt around her waist. "I have this Magic Belt and it's no trick for it to send a note for me to anywhere I want it to."

At that the other girls laughed and Dorothy exclaimed, "On the other hand, it's quite a trick!"

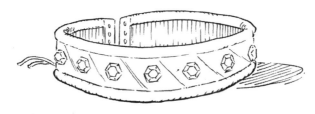

Chapter 3
Off to the Mountains

t was simple to send the message. Ozma took Chris up to her own magnificent apartment in the Palace. There she took out a piece of her engraved stationary and wrote on it:

Dear Mr. & Mrs. Pedersen,

I have invited Chris to spend a few days with me. I am sure she will enjoy herself and will be quite safe. We will make certain that she is back at her Uncle Walt's house the day before Christmas Eve. We are enjoying her being with us. Thank you.

Sincerely,
Ozma of Oz

Christmas in Oz

At the bottom, Chris wrote:

Dear Mom & Dad,
I can't believe this is happening, but it re-
ally is true. I'm in Oz! There is something really
magic about that old Lucky Umbrella after all.
I love you all, and I'll see you in a few days with
a lot to tell you!

Love,
Chris

It was nearly nine by now and Chris was sure her family would already be worried about her, so just to be sure that they would receive the note and understand that it was real, Ozma said, "Let's watch this in the Magic Picture," and led the way over to a large picture of a blue Munchkin field. Standing in front of it, Ozma said, "Show us Chris's mother in Philadelphia, Pennsylvania, U. S. A."

Without hesitation, the picture changed to the inside of a house. Sure enough, it was Aunt Lydia's kitchen and there were Chris's mother, father, Uncle Walt and Aunt Lydia. They were talking with lively animation but looking quite worried. Her mother had just started to reach for a cup of tea when Ozma, with one hand on her Magic Belt and the note in her other hand, said, "Put this note in the outreaching hand of Chris's mother."

And there, in her mother's hand, was their little let-

Off to the Mountains

ter. She jerked her hand back and dropped the piece of paper to the floor.

"What's that?" she exclaimed.

"Where did you get it?" asked her husband.

"I don't know. I was reaching for my teacup when, all of a sudden, there that piece of paper was in my hand."

Uncle Walt bent over and picked up the strange piece of paper, looked at it and then handed it to Chris's mother, saying, "Here. It is addressed to you two."

She glanced at it. Gasped. Laughed. Then said, "This must be some kind of a joke! I can't believe it. But it surely arrived as if by magic." Then she read it to everyone.

Excited talk followed. Watching them, Chris said, "It may take them awhile to figure this all out, but I think they'll soon do so."

"Time for us to leave then," said Ozma and she led the way back down to rejoin the others in front of the Palace. Once there, she made four assignments.

The first was to send Cap'n Bill out the East Gate toward the Munchkin Country. There, somewhere along the Yellow Brick Road, he would meet Uncle Henry Aunt Em and Scraps touring in the Red Wagon pulled by the Wooden Sawhorse. That one-time carpenter's sawhorse had been brought to life by Ozma in one of her earliest adventures. Even if they had to go quite a way, the Sawhorse was capable of such great speed that they should certainly get to Viridian Mountain by the next day.

The Wizard and Tik-Tok would stay in the Emerald City and join Ozma's group later. The Wizard was the first Earth person to immigrate to Oz. He had been a balloonist and magician for a circus, but had been blown off course, ending up in the middle of Oz. Between his magic tricks and the fact that he had descended from the sky in a balloon with the letters "OZ" emblazoned on its side, it was easy to convince the Oz people that he was a Wizard.

Tik-Tok was a mechanical man that Dorothy had

Off to the Mountains

found in a cave on her second visit to Oz. He stood upon two very short, flexible copper legs that supported his body which was a large sphere of hollow copper, containing the clockwork that made him move and think and talk. On top of his body was a big round copper head with a removable copper hat. Those short legs dictated a slow pace, so rather than slow everyone, he and the Wizard would stay in the Emerald City, leaving the next morning. Then they would use some of the Wizard's magic to land near the top of Scarlet Mountain. They would then be on the far side of the mysterious valley from where Ozma's group would have spent

Christmas in Oz

the night at Springer's home by Viridian Springs.

Ozma left Omby Amby, the Soldier with the Green Whiskers, in charge of the affairs of state while she was gone. He was highest ranking officer in the Army of Oz, a Captain-General. Indeed, he was the entire Army of Oz, and it had been so long since he had used the ancient musket he carried that he always had a bouquet of flowers in its muzzle. Besides, he always said, "Flowers are better. If I had it loaded with bullets, someone might get hurt."

Ozma, herself, would lead all the rest of her close friends from the palace up to Springer's place at Viridian Springs. They would spend the night there and then go on up to the top of Viridian Mountain the next morning.

Once all these announcements had been made, it took only a few minutes to clear the driveway, as each party set out upon its own particular journey. As Ozma's group approached the South Gate of the city, a young boy came running out of a side street. "Ah, I've found you," he said. "I was afraid you were all lost," and he fell into step with the others, although his step was more of a skip.

"So there you are Button-Bright," said Trot.

"No, it's not us who have been lost," said Dorothy.

"Might even have been you," growled the Cowardly Lion.

Button-Bright stuck his tongue out at the Lion, but

Off to the Mountains

continued walking peacefully with the others. Only a few steps later he tugged on the umbrella in Chris's hand and said, "Hey, where'd you get my umbrella?"

"Your's!" she exclaimed. "This is my Great-Uncle Walt's."

Looking closer, Button-Bright countered, "Naw, that's mine all right. I would recognize that elephant handle anywhere. I haven't seen it in years, not since I lost it in the popcorn snow of Mo."

A little annoyed by his attitude, Chris replied, "I'll have you know, young man, this has been in our family for a lot longer than that. It is our good luck piece and has been handed down from father to son for generations and generations.

"Ha! That's the same with my umbrella," said Button-Bright. "What's your full name?"

Leaning over, she whispered in his ear, "It's Merrie Christmas Pederson, but don't you dare call me that. I can't stand that silly name. I was born on Christmas Day, so my folks thought it would be cute to name me Merrie Christmas! My family usually just calls me 'Christmas,' but I still think that's a little strange. You can't imagine the teasing I got from other kids, so I just go by 'Chris.'"

"Oh yes, I can imagine. I was just a little boy, but I had already been ribbed about my nickname, Button-Bright. But that was better than having them know my real name."

Christmas in Oz

Chris said, "What's your real name?"

Still whispering, Button-Bright said, "Saladin Paracelsus de Lambertine Evagne von Smith." Then, sounding rather disappointed, he added, "and I guess that proves it's not the same umbrella after all. None of my names sound anything like any part of yours."

"But," cried Chris, jumping up and down in her excitement, "von Smith is my Uncle's last name and I never heard of anyone since the Crusades who was named Saladin other than his long lost older brother. And you say this is you umbrella, so you must be my long lost Great-Uncle Saladin!"

Off to the Mountains

As she spoke, the entire group stopped and looked at the two children who stood there, silently looking at each other.

It was Dorothy who broke the silence, exclaiming, "You mean you're related to each other, really?"

And Trot said, "Then you must know where Button-Bright lives and who his family is. We didn't know if he even had any relatives."

"I guess he does," said Chris, "since I seem to be one of them and I've just come from his family home."

"Uh, is the house a big old one in Philadelphia?" asked the little boy. "Three floors and an attic above that?"

"That's it – big and old. But the umbrella has been in that house for ages and ages, so how did you get here?"

"That was exactly it" said Button-Bright, "ages and ages ago I rode it to Mo and landed in a big drift of pop-corn. Trot and Cap'n Bill pulled me out, but we couldn't find the umbrella anyplace and that's the last I saw of it until now. But the real question is how did it get back to Philadelphia when I lost it in Mo?"

"That is strange, but Uncle Walt did say that you and it both disappeared at the same time. But then a few days later the umbrella was back in its regular place in the attic, and no one ever saw you again. Now I know why.

"Wow, won't Uncle Walt be surprised when he hears that I've found his long lost brother! You have been missing ever since before he was born, and he's eighty-five now."

Everyone thought it quite a coincidence that Button-Bright's grandniece should show up and here she was three years older than he. Conversation about it continued for quite a while with Button-Bright finding out as much about his family as he could and Chris hearing about all her great uncle's adventures, both in and out of Oz.

Eventually other subjects came up and the group continued making good time as they wended their way south.

Chris was totally engrossed in the experience. The greenness reminded her of her home in the Puget Sound Country, even to the approaching rugged mountains. But there were so many ways in which Oz was different from anything she had ever known before. Everyone was so friendly and unafraid. People they met greeted them casually, with little of the deference one would expect with the Queen of the land in the party. Indeed, when they were passing a farmhouse just before noon, the children playing in front ran inside to get their mother. Dusting flour from her hands, the trim and sprightly young mother said, "Welcome to our home. I was just finishing preparations for our lunch and we would be most happy to have you stop to help us eat it."

Speaking for her group, Ozma said, "Your invitation

Off to the Mountains

honors us. But we don't want to be any bother, so if you will, with a wave of my wand I can make whatever you prepare for your own family become enough to feed all of us."

The good lady seemed satisfied with that, so while she and Ozma went back to the kitchen to finish preparations, the others got acquainted with the children. Soon a veritable feast was before them, enjoyed by all, but they dared not linger. So, not long after lunch was over, they were on their way and now headed more to the southeast. After a while Chris said to her companions, "I just can't believe all this. There really is an Oz,

Christmas in Oz

and here I am right in the middle of one of your exciting adventures! Wow! What a story I will have to tell when I get back to Uncle Walt's! But how'll I ever get the kids back home to believe me?"

"No one ever believed me!" exclaimed Button-Bright.

"Well, you are naturally a little unbelievable anyway," declared the Hungry Tiger.

But Trot came to his defense, saying, "Cap'n Bill and I had some magical adventures before we ever came to Oz, and no one back home would believe us, and Cap'n Bill was even an adult."

"Yes," said Dorothy. "It's just hard to get people to believe what they don't want to believe."

"But, I bet Chris believes in Oz now," purred the Cowardly Lion.

"I always did," replied Chris. "It always seemed very real, but not accessible. Now, I know it's real and accessible."

Toward evening they arrived at Springer's cottage, and Ozma began preparations for dinner. In such a fairyland, that was quite simple. Ozma just waved her wand over some chips of wood and there were tables and chairs for everyone. Then she had each person place a handful of rocks on the table and with another wave of her wand, the table was spread with plates, silverware and crystal goblets and large silver pans upon the low table for the animals. Finally, she took a small packet from the pack she carried, sprinkled its contents across

Off to the Mountains

the tables, waved her wand and immediately each plate was full of steaming hot food, the goblets were filled with delicious cool drinks and the right food was in the pans before each of the animals.

While they were eating, Chris kept glancing at Ozma. Finally the Queen held out her hands to her and said, "Come here Chris dear. Something about me seems to be mystifying you."

"Well, yes. You see, I had never read any of the Oz books until just a few days ago. And when I read about how you came to your throne, I thought it said you were a blonde."

"Why, you're quite right. When I first became Queen I certainly was a blonde. But then I started wearing these red poppies in my hair all the time, and I just thought they would look better if my hair was black."

"Oh! You dye it then?" Laughing, Ozma replied, "My goodness. No! I'm a fairy. I don't need artificial color. See, I just wave my wand," and as she did so, her long black hair was suddenly golden yellow. Everyone at the tables gasped a bit for most of them had never seen her as a blonde.

"Surprise!" exclaimed Ozma. "You didn't know I was really a blond, did you? Maybe I should leave it this way?" As there were more gasps, she quickly added, "No. I'm just joking. I've had black hair too long to go back to blonde now." To Chris, she added, "I don't usually dabble in this kind of magic, but you seemed genu-

Christmas in Oz

inely concerned about what had happened to my hair. Besides, I thought my friends might like to know what I would look like if I hadn't changed my hair color. From their response, I think they agree with me. I'll stay a brunette." With another wave of her wand, her hair was once more pitch black.

When everyone had eaten his or her fill, she used her wand again, and all the dishes were gone.

"The tables and chairs we can continue to use," said the young Queen, "and when bedtime comes we will all be similarly supplied with tents, beds, bedding and night clothes. So enjoy the evening!"

And they did.

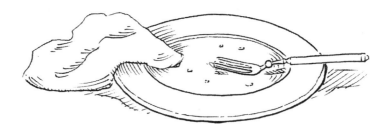

CHAPTER 4
The Wicked Blue Witch of the East

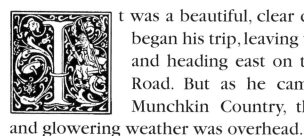t was a beautiful, clear day as Cap'n Bill began his trip, leaving the Emerald City and heading east on the Yellow Brick Road. But as he came close to the Munchkin Country, the sky clouded and glowering weather was overhead.

He had not gone far into the Munchkin Country when he saw a little old lady sitting in front of a cottage by the side of the road. She wore the blue clothing typical of the Munchkins, although a much darker blue than usual. Then, instead of the usual bonnet and peasant dress of a Munchkin woman, she had on a high peaked hat and a long, flowing gown. Her pointed shoes curled up at the end as usual, but it was all in such a very dark blue. And her typically domed house was also in that

Christmas in Oz

same dark blue.

"Hello, my good woman," said the old sailor, "have you seen a Red Wagon pulled by a Wooden Sawhorse and carrying an older couple with a life-size Patchwork Girl?"

"Ha, don't call me 'good'," she responded as she stood up, revealing that she was not one of the little Munchkins from the central part of Munchkinland. "I am Lorabie, the Wicked Blue Witch of the East, and I'm going to conquer all of Oz because no one gives me the recognition I deserve."

Now Cap'n Bill thought that all the wicked witches were gone, but after eighty years of stomping around Oz, he was used to all sorts of strange things happening, so he merely replied, "Pleased to meet you, ma'am. I am Cap'n Bill Weedles."

"Ha, you don't have to tell me. I know who you are. My mystical powers are very great!"

"Well, then," he answered smoothly, "I suppose you can tell me how long before I will meet my friends."

"Ha, I can, but I won't! What I will tell you is that you will find them on this very road to the east of here, and you will soon run into trouble as a result! Goodbye!" And she folded her arms across her chest and looked very sternly at him.

Just then a low growl was heard from the house and two bright spots of light appeared in the shadowy doorway. From the dark interior emerged a very large

The Wicked Blue Witch of the East

black leopard. "Every witch should have a black cat," said Lorabie, "and this is mine. Midnight is her name."

"Ah yes. Well, goodbye, then," and offering them a tip of his cap, Cap'n Bill turned and started on up the road. It was about half an hour before he rounded a corner and saw the Sawhorse pulling the Red Wagon toward him. After greetings were exchanged, Cap'n Bill told the others, "Ozma has taken a group to Viridian Springs to investigate a mystery and we are to join them up in the valley between Scarlet Mountain and Viridian Mountain just as soon as we can."

"Well, I certainly can't pull this wagon through the

woods on that narrow trail up beyond Springer's," complained the Sawhorse.

"That's OK," responded Cap'n Bill, "I know of an old road going up Viridian Mountain from the east. It isn't used much, but there should be plenty of room for the Red Wagon to get through."

By this time the clouds had grown darker and more threatening, so he hopped quickly into the spacious and comfortable Red Wagon, and the Sawhorse pulled it around so they could head west on the Yellow Brick Road.

They were moving quite rapidly and in a few minutes were back to Lorabie's cottage, when suddenly the Sawhorse stumbled, the wagon tipped over and its occupants were rolled upon the ground. There was a cackling laugh from behind the bushes and up stood Lorabie, saying, "Ha, my doubting friends. How do you like a little taste of my magic?"

"Not very much," responded Cap'n Bill as everyone tried to determine what the damages were. It turned out that the only real trouble was with the Wooden Sawhorse and the Red Wagon. The horse had a broken leg, which is why he had tipped everything over in the first place, and the Wagon had two broken wheels.

"Now that wasn't very nice of you!" exclaimed Uncle Henry. "We didn't do anything to hurt you."

"No, but you would have if you had had the chance. You are no different from anyone else. Besides, you

The Wicked Blue Witch of the East

don't believe I'm a Witch, do you?"

"I don't know about that," answered Cap'n Bill, "but you sure act like one."

Uncle Henry had already begun poking around in the road and now he said, "Truth is, I sure don't believe you're a real witch! Look here. You've drilled holes all around in this here road and covered 'em with cloth and a thin layer of dirt. That's not magic. It's just plain mischievous mechanics."

Lorabie answered, "Ha, that's all you know! This is the way stumbling magic is done. You are used to that simple little Ozma and ridiculous Glinda and that humbug Wizard who don't really know how these things are done. It takes training and study and practice to get it right. Ha, I'll show you real magic! You don't believe I know what I'm doing. Ha, I'll make it rain for you."

With that the old witch retired into her cottage and soon returned with an armful of paraphernalia which she deposited upon the ground. From the stack she drew forth a rug and smoothed it out upon the grass and began arranging the other items around its edges. Sitting in the midst of it all, she said, "Ha, now let me teach you a thing or two.

"First of all, this is sympathetic magic. We want rain, so we do something that is like rain. Ha! Now I need to concentrate, so I will ask you to be silent while I work my magic."

Then she began a strange ritual. While she moved

Christmas in Oz

things around, she kept up a constant chant of mumbled phrases, none of which made any sense to anyone else. At last, she picked up a copper kettle with various mystic designs etched upon its surface, poured its contents into a large bowl and, reaching her hands into the bowl, started sprinkling the water around her. First she sprinkled it to the north, then to the south, then to the east, and then to the west. Finally, she threw the remnants of the water high into the air as she spun around and around, yelling over and over, "Rain, rain, come today. Now's the time for rainy play!"

After she stopped, everyone stood around a few

The Wicked Blue Witch of the East

minutes while she gathered up the tools she had been using. When she was done, Aunt Em said, "Now that was a right pretty show, but where's the rain?"

"Ha, you people just don't know. Go ahead, make fun while you can. But just wait. The rain will be here soon, never fear!"

"In that case," exclaimed Uncle Henry, as he began rummaging around in the Red Wagon, "we'd better hurry and get the Sawhorse and the Wagon repaired!"

While Cap'n Bill cut a branch to make a new leg for the Sawhorse, Uncle Henry started on the wheels. Both of them were handy at repairs, using the tools in a large box under the back seat, they were able to get right to work. Nonetheless, it took several hours before everything was done. Plus they needed to stop midway in their jobs to share the lunch Aunt Em had packed in the wagon. All in all, it was midafternoon by the time they had finished and cleaned everything up, including filling in all the holes the dreadful witch had drilled in the road. They were just climbing back into the wagon, when it began to rain.

Hobbling toward them from her house, Lorabie cried out happily, "Ha, you didn't believe me did you? Now you'll believe! This is the rain I ordered up!" Then wrapping her cape close around her, she called over her shoulder, "Kitty, kitty, kitty!"

Almost immediately Midnight appeared at the doorway of the round little house, languidly stretching. Then

Christmas in Oz

looking at those in the wagon, he licked his chops and said, "Which one first?"

"No, no my pet. Not yet, at least. We simply have some traveling to do," and with that, she jumped upon his back and away they ran, across the fields to the southwest with the rain sprinkling lightly upon them.

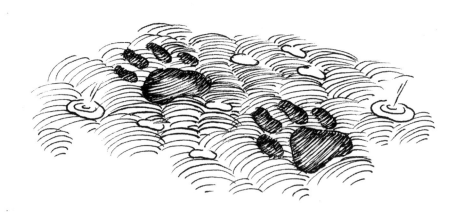

Chapter 5
Christmas Valley

hat in tarnation!" exclaimed Uncle Henry, "I didn't think there were any Wicked Witches left in the Land of Oz."

"I didn't either," responded Aunt Em. "But I guess she sho 'nuff is one."

"Looked like one. Talked like one. Acted like one. That's enough for me," declared the Sawhorse. "That was just a plain mean trick she pulled on me."

"And all of us," added Aunt Em.

The Sawhorse continued taking them through the light rain at a rapid pace along the Yellow Brick Road. By the time they reached the second side road to the south west, the rain had stopped. They continued on up that road and, at last, when they came to the top of an especially steep hill they could see tall and rug-

Christmas in Oz

ged mountains rising to the west under the still heavily overcast skies. Our friends could not help wondering, for the mountains were covered with snow, a thing unheard of in Oz.

"Whoa now. What are we getting into?" asked Uncle Henry.

"Snow on the mountains!" exclaimed Aunt Em.

"But why stop now?" the Sawhorse asked in a critical voice.

"No one told you to stop," answered the Patchwork Girl.

"Uncle Henry said, 'Whoa,' and that sounds like 'Stop' to me," replied the horse.

"I didn't mean it like that. It was just a way of saying that I was surprised."

"Crazy humans," muttered the horse, unheard by any of the others, "can't tell the difference between stopping and being surprised!"

"Guess I didn't mention the snow, did I?" said Cap'n Bill. "That seemed the least of the problems Springer mentioned and, by comparison, hardly seemed like news worth repeating."

"What do ya mean?" asked Aunt Em. "Nothin' you've said so far sounds so terrible."

"Hain't said much, yet," said the old sailor. "Truth is, up in the valley 'tween Viridian and Scarlet Mountains, a strange village has shown up. No one rightly knows how it got there or where it came from. Then there's

this Lorabie. She's put cursing signs all over those mountains. 'Peers to me that she might be causin' more trouble than you'd think."

After a few more words about it, the Sawhorse drew them up to an even more magnificent vista than before and the irrepressible Scraps bounced out of the wagon, saying, "It is so beautiful. It makes me want to make up a poem, but even poetry cannot do justice to such beauty as this."

"Yup," responded Uncle Henry, "ya know, I was just thinkin.' Back on Earth we had travel books, an' I remember some pictures of a place called Switzerland.

Christmas in Oz

Oh, that was supposed to have 'bout the most beautiful mountains in the world, but sure as tootin' they couldn't beat these!"

"And even if it is unexpected," laughed Scraps, "I'm glad the snow is there. It's half the beauty."

"Sure! And when we get into that snow pretty soon, see how well you like it," quipped the Sawhorse. "You'll just get your cotton stuffing all wet and soggy."

They continued and late in the afternoon, they reached the snow, then the pass that marked the top of their trip through the mountains. And there they saw the threatening message:

"THIS WILL NEVER BE.
CURSED MAY IT BE,
AND ALL BECAUSE OF ME.
SO SAYS LORABIE!"

"Land o' Goshen" declared Aunt Em. "Just like you said, a threat from that dratted Lorabie."

"What will never be? And what will be cursed," asked Scraps.

"The very thing I asked when Springer first told us 'bout these signs," explained Cap'n Bill, "an' we still don't have any idea what she's talkin' 'bout."

By this time, the sun was getting ready to set, and looking down into the valley beyond the pass which they saw was completely blanketed in show. The encircling and towering mountains were now tipped in pink by the setting sun. Below them the landsape was gradually growing darker and darker. In the middle of the valley stood a quaint little village whose chimneys wreathed it in smoke and whose light shone from every window. For a few minutes all stood quietly and motionless, overcome by the peaceful beauty of the scene.

Finally, it was Scraps who broke the silence:

"My, oh my. What have we here?
A town, a village does appear.
Covered 'round about with snow
That on the valley casts a glow.
'Tis so quaint, so beautiful.
It really does your eye fill full."

In amazement, Uncle Henry declared, "Thunderation! How can this be?" And as he slapped Cap'n Bill on the back, he added, "You told us so, but always before this has been a deserted area!"

"And snow in Oz is just unheard of," insisted Aunt Em.

"But Oz is full of the unheard of," laughed Cap'n Bill. "I still do not like it," complained the Sawhorse. "It just is not right. First that witch, then this snow, the message and now that mysterious town."

Suddenly, out of the air in front of them a voice

spoke, "Ah ha, but snow around Christmas Valley is a good thing."

As they watched the spot from which the voice was coming, the form of a little man began to appear. Then another and another and more popped into sight until seven strange little men stood before them. Six were elves. The toes of their boots curled up, and the peaked tips of their hats curled down. Pointed ears poked out from beneath their hats, and each little elf wore a wide brown leather belt around his waist. Each was dressed all in one shade, and each one differed from the other. The first was in light blue, another in rose, one in

Christmas Valley

brown, another in dark green, the fifth in a light silver-gray, and the last in light green.

The seventh little man was darker and taller than the others, but bent and gnarled. He was dressed in the fine garb of the olden days, with short, puffy pants and a tight sleeveless jacket. These were made of bright red and green striped velvet. His shirt was of white silk with embroidered sleeves and a stiffened ruff at the neck. Tight green leggings led down to soft red leather shoes. A short cape of red and green satin was loosely thrown over his shoulders. All was topped off by a jaunty, jeweled green beret with an ostrich feather stuck in it. A gold chain hung across the front of his jacket, and he carried a slender birch rod in his hand.

"Peter!" cried Aunt Em, "What are you doing here?" Reaching over to shake the little man's hand, Uncle Henry beamed as he asked, "Why Peter, you old scalawag! Yes, what are you doing here?"

Bowing low, the little man answered, "Santa Claus sent us out to welcome you to Christmas Valley. He has been expecting you."

"You mean Santa Claus is down there!" exclaimed Cap'n Bill.

"I always thought he lived in the Laughing Valley of Hohaho," added Scraps.

"Or the North Pole," continued Uncle Henry.

"Yes, on Earth it is the North Pole, and in Oz, it is the Valley of Hohaho," answered Peter, "but from now on he will be spending a lot of time right here."

"Why does he want to do a thing like that?" asked the Patchwork Girl.

"It is no mystery," replied Peter, "but I will let Santa be the one to tell you all about it."

"That is a good idea," grumbled the Sawhorse. "Then we will not have to stand around here all day," and, turning his head toward his friends, he added with a wry smile, "Giddap!"

With that, they all started out, Peter leading the way. He had been one of Santa's chief helpers from the beginning, and had accompanied the jolly old man to a number of parties in the Emerald City. The little elves, however, were all new acquaintances for the five travelers, so as they started down into the valley, Peter introduced them in the order in which they had first appeared as Bubbles, Birdswing, Riddles, Skydew, Thistledown and Billy-Billy Bleep-Bleep.

Conversation then trailed off into silence as the visitors looked around themselves, enjoying the wintry splendor. Even their caravan added to the landscape, helping to make it an idyllic winter scene. The bright little elves, with Peter leading the way and the Sawhorse pulling his four friends, made a moving line of color in the expanse of white that lay stretched across the valley. In the midst of the vale, they headed for the village, with its big brown buildings, yellow lights still gleaming through the windows against the gray

Christmas Valley

skies of this morning, and soft blue-gray smoke drifting from the chimneys. Occasional trees were dark-footed mounds in the midst of the frosty landscape. All set off by the sharply beautiful outlines of the snowy mountains. As might be expected, Scraps was the first to break from the enchantment of the beauty. Riding along, she reached out, quickly sweeping some snow off a branch and tossing it over her shoulder into Uncle Henry's face. Although taken by surprise, he was quick to respond by wiping the remnants off his face and forming it into a snowball to squash on the Patchwork Girl's head.

However, before he could complete his project, Scraps called out, "Hey, that wasn't even wet. Look at me, you smart old Sawhorse. The snow did not get my cotton hands the least bit wet!"

The wooden horse snorted at that remark but did not deign to say a thing. He really had no chance to do so, for almost immediately Uncle Henry spoke up: "Sakes alive, would ya look at that. It's not even cold! See. I've kept ahold of this snow on top of Scraps' head and my hands are just as warm as ever they could be."

"Right as light, and not a melt in sight," observed Scraps.

"Of course not," remarked Peter. "You all know there is no natural snow here. This is unnatural snow."

"This snow, and I'll bet the snow on those mountains, too, is artificial, eh?" said Uncle Henry.

Christmas in Oz

"So it is," replied Birdswing, the brown clad elf. "With this kind of snow we have all the advantages of real snow and none of the disadvantages. See how beautiful it looks, and you can throw snowballs and make snowmen and go sledding in it, yet you never get wet or cold."

By this time they had reached the village and were approaching the largest building. Like all the others, it had a steeply sloping roof and was of charming Alpine construction. Crossed beams of wood and stucco-covered bricks formed the outer walls. Ends of a number of the buildings were painted with fanciful scenes in bright colors. This largest one was decorated with a great and beautifully trimmed Christmas tree design with all kinds of children dancing around it, flooded with bright rays of light from the tree.

Just as Uncle Henry was remarking on how appealing the scene was, the front door burst open and out strode the real, live Santa Claus.

"Well dad-burned! If it isn't Mr. Claus, himself!" exclaimed Uncle Henry.

"Santa," cried Scraps, as all four hopped from the carriage.

Standing on the doorstep of the Inn, old acquaintances were quickly renewed. Then the visitors turned to follow Santa inside. Doing so was just like walking into a Swiss chalet at Christmas time. The rooms were big and high with open woodwork everywhere. There

Christmas Valley

was a spacious entry hall with a curved stairway coming down the far side from a balcony on the second floor. A huge decorated Christmas tree towered in the wide sweeping curve of the stairs. Smaller ones stood in each corner of the hall and garlands of evergreen and tinsel festooned the walls.

Santa led them to the end of the hall where it opened into a large room with a cheery fire burning in a big fireplace. Like the entry hall, this room was decorated for Christmas with another large tree right in the middle of the front window. Holly wreathes hung on the walls with garlands of greenery looping between them. Tinsel strands draped from the walls to the large oaken chandelier in the center of the room. A hundred flickering candles upon it cast their light into every corner of the room. The large wooden beams that stretched across the room contrasted with heavy darkness against the brightness of all the greenery and colorful decorations. As they walked under the chandelier, Cap'n Bill grabbed Scraps and kissed her soundly on her cotton stuffed cheek. When he let go, she somersaulted herself into a sitting position on the floor and twirled around to look at the others, saying:

"My sakes alive,
What's happening here?
He's lost his mind
I certainly fear."

Christmas in Oz

By this time everyone was laughing as Santa, pointing above the Patchwork Girl to the chandelier, said, "I'm surprised your button bright eyes did not pick out the mistletoe hanging there."

"My eyes may be bright as buttons," quipped Scraps, "but I guess it is Cap'n Bill that has the sharp eyes."

"It pays to be sharp eyed," he laughed and sat upon a hassock near the fireplace. The others sought out their own comfortable seats around that same fireplace and settled down to talk with Santa of days gone by.

Chapter 6

Beside the Fireplace

 s soon as the travelers were settled, elves began coming in with trays heaped with Christmas cheer for their guests. There was marzipan, candied orange peel, snickerdoodles, speculaas, fruit cake, and sugar cookies in the shape of Santa's, reindeer and trees, plus pitchers full of red or green punch. It was a happy evening for all those gathered beside Santa's big fireplace. He told them about his hectic, swift as light trips around the world on Christmas Eve and the busy times in his workshops throughout the year.

"Eh, you say 'workshops'!" exclaimed Uncle Henry. "I thought you just had one at the North Pole."

So Santa explained how that was true in Mortal Lands, but here, in the Fairy Realms, his original home

Christmas in Oz

and workshop had always been in the Laughing Valley of Hohaho. Now both of these workshops had been working at capacity for many years and he needed a newer, bigger more modern facility or he would never be able to keep up with the needs of the children of two worlds.

After thinking about a variety of possibilities he had decided that, if Ozma would approve, he would like to locate in the red and green borderland between the Quadlings and the Emerald City. Of course, she had been enthusiastic, so the two, after much secret searching in the past August, had chosen this particular location as Christmas Valley. It was high and secluded and in the rugged eastern mountains separating the two countries. With its high mountains, this unnatural snow would at least seem logical.

When Santa said that Ozma and he had chosen this place in August, Uncle Henry exclaimed, "August! So that's what all those mysterious goings on were about! Ozma was gone for days at a time with never a word about it and all questions answered with merely, 'You will find out later.'"

"And now it is later, and we have found out, all right," laughed Scraps.

"Ho, ho," laughed Santa, "that's right, although things have worked out a little differently than we had planned. Ozma was just going to bring you up here saying she had a big surprise for you on top of Viridian Mountain.

Beside the Fireplace

Then two nights ago she arrived by Magic Belt to tell me about the messages on the rocks, and we decided that would be reason enough to bring you all to Christmas Valley." So here we are, and tomorrow when the others join us, we will have a big party!"

"Hooray!" his guests shouted as they turned again to Santa to hear more about his plans for Christmas Valley. Headquarters and his personal home would still be at the North Pole, but this idealized little Christmas village would serve as a major center for making some of the toys.

As a matter of fact, the reindeer really preferred the North Pole, for it had something Oz would probably never have. You would think that after centuries of Arctic silence, they would be disturbed by the noise of the modern jets. But, actually, since these airplanes were the only things on earth that could even approach the speed of the reindeer, they said it was something like having big, noisy cousins flying by. The roar when they sped overhead was just like a friendly "Hello." However, as with all the others, they were also thrilled with their part-time home in Oz.

Scraps and the Wooden Sawhorse, of course, needed no sleep. So, when the others retired to their beds upstairs, they simply stayed downstairs all night, enjoying the abundant Christmas atmosphere of the inn.

From time to time throughout the night, various ones of Santa's helpers dropped in to talk with them.

Christmas in Oz

In this way, the two visitors learned much more about who was here and what they were doing.

Santa Claus had brought some of each kind of his helpers. Besides the reindeer, there were four other groups that had also been close friends and helpers of his since the beginning: elves, ryls, wood nymphs and knooks.

Most of us know about elves magical people, dainty and small of stature, blithe of spirit, specialists in various crafts. With Santa were toy-making elves, cooking elves, general maintenance elves, recording elves, decorating elves and elves of all kinds.

But there were two areas outside the elves care. These were the animals and the greenery which were the special responsibility of the three lesser known groups of sprites.

Since life began, ryls had been taking care of flowers. Here, in Christmas Valley, this primarily meant poinsettias and mistletoe were the chief concern of these merry little elf-sized men.

Wood nymphs had come here with Santa to tend the trees. They trimmed trees and cut Christmas greenery from holly and other evergreens. These little ladies were delightful beings about the size of the elves and the ryls.

Taller than the others, though still smaller than an average mortal, the bent and gnarled knooks were somber of nature, sometimes even a bit gruff. Guardians of

Beside the Fireplace

animals all around the world, those in Christmas Valley were here to care for Santa's reindeer. Their leader, Peter, had been one of Santa's first four immortal helpers, travelling with him throughout the worlds from the beginning.

Although the elves were specialists in toy-making, there were wood nymph and ryls and knooks who helped when it came to working with wood or making toy plants and animals. By working throughout the year, these fairy folk would have their quota of toys and gifts prepared by Christmas time. In general, the things prepared in one workshop were for delivery in that area,

Christmas in Oz

but Christmas Valley produced many special toys that were needed everywhere, so these had to be taken to the other workshops weeks ahead of time. There they would be ready for Santa to pick them up and deliver them all around both worlds on his Christmas Eve trips.

After they had learned much about Santa's expanding operations, the Patchwork Girl and the Wooden Sawhorse were pleased to see the six little elves that had greeted them on the hillside coming in to enjoy the smoldering embers of the fire.

"When it is like this." said Birdswing, "it reminds me of looking down into the stomach of a sleeping dragon."

"You've never looked into one," grumbled Thistledown.

"Well, that is what I think it would look like anyway."

"I do not like to think much about fire," commented Scraps. For a lady of my composition, it is a dangerous subject."

"For me too," added the Sawhorse.

So Scraps changed the subject by satisfying her curiosity about Billy-Billy Bleep-Bleep's name. Why was it so different from those of the other elves?

"It's really not so different," he explained. "Like all elfin names, it has something to do with my trade."

"Now what trade has anything to do with billy-billy bleep-bleep?" was the Sawhorse's rather sarcastic question.

Beside the Fireplace

"That is easier to explain than you might think," laughed the little elf. "As a youngster, before I had a trade, I was simply called 'Billy'. Growing up, I developed a talent for mechanical things. The toys I crafted usually made noises something like 'bleep-bleep.' Now, that did not make a very good name in itself. So, where most elves change their name when they adopt a trade, I just added on to mine. It did not take my friends long to start doubling the first part of my name, too. So, here I am today: Billy-Billy Bleep-Bleep."

Laughing then, Scraps cried out, "Let me guess about the others. Riddles, I'll bet works on puzzles."

"And tricks and all such," added the dark green-clad elf, "and your patchwork makes me think you might be good at figuring out some of my puzzles."

"Bubbles, then, must make balloons and other stretchy things," she continued.

"Exactly right," responded Bubbles.

"Then, I suppose Thistledown goes around punching holes in your balloons," remarked the Sawhorse, neighing his funny little laugh.

"You are thinking of the wrong part of my name," answered that little elf. "It's the second half. I stuff things with down or feathers or sawdust or cotton, things like teddy bears or pillows or dolls."

"That makes you my kind of elf!" laughed Scraps, patting her own stuffing. Then, turning to the last two elves, she continued, "And I bet that Birdswing and Skydew work with flying toys."

"That's my job, all right," was the rose-clad elf's reply.

Skydew, however, said, "Ah-hah, you will have to guess again about my job. Like Thistledown, it is the last part of my name that is the clue."

"Skydew? Does that mean you do all sorts of things?" asked the stuffed girl.

"No, no, no," replied the little elf. "I am an elfin cook, for it is things like the dew of the morning and honey-suckle juice that is our food."

So the night passed as the girl of cloth and the horse of wood talked with these and others of Santa's help-ers. By morning they felt they had learned a great deal about Christmas Valley and those who worked there.

Chapter 7

Viridian Mountain

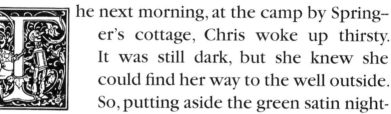

he next morning, at the camp by Spring-er's cottage, Chris woke up thirsty. It was still dark, but she knew she could find her way to the well outside. So, putting aside the green satin night-gown she had found under her pillow the night before, she dressed quickly and quietly so as not to awaken the other girls in her tent. When she reached the well, she found the water cold, but sweet and good.

Standing there, enjoying the taste, she could see that dawn was on its way. Soon it began to touch the eastern sky with pink color, gradually moving across the sky, light pink gradually increasing to a more rosette hue, spreading from the far edge of the sky to tint the fluffy clouds and touch the nearby mountains with its

Christmas in Oz

deepening color.

As the rising sun changed the early reds to golden yellow, Chris moved away from the well. The cool, fresh mountain air was exhilarating and she started to hike through the trees, up the mountain with occasional views out across Oz, growing wider and more breathtaking. Chris knew better than to be out of earshot from the others, and soon turned back toward Springer's cabin. No sooner did she do so than two dark forms materialized out of the woods.

"Good morning to you, young lady," said one. "I am the Blue Witch of the East, Lorabie, and," indicating the great cat beside her, "this is my friend, Midnight."

"Oh! Good morning. You startled me," Chris replied, trying to keep her voice from shaking and trying to be polite at the same time. "I am Chris Pederson from Olympia."

"Ha! Yes, of course you are. Did you think I, the great Lorabie, did not already know that?"

"Lorabie? Aren't you the one that left the message on the stone in the pass?"

"Ha! Yes, messages! One at each pass leading into that valley; public notices of the doom to come!" And with ever increasing vehemence, she continued, "It is my duty to rid the world of that abomination being placed in the valley. You'll see! I'll make it disappear just like that!" and she snapped her fingers.

As she said "abomination," she pulled a coin from a

pocket in her gown and held it out in her right hand for Chris to see. Then she passed her left hand over her right, and at the word "that," showed her right hand with no coin in it and then her left, also empty.

"My goodness," laughed Chris. "You do that even better than my dad does. You're just too hard to follow."

"Ha," answered Lorabie, "You don't take me seriously do you? You'll be sorry!"

"But I do take you seriously," answered Chris.

"I tried to be friendly with you," continued the old witch as though she had not even heard the young girl, "and where did it get me? You're just like all the rest!

Christmas in Oz

You enjoy Christmas while I get left out. All of you think Christmas is so important! Well, this is the end of it. I will soon be rid of that fat old man and all his stupid cohorts."

With that, she jumped upon Midnight's back, raised her hand, said, "Farewell!" and as she dropped her hand to her side, there was a flash, a bang, and she was swallowed in a great puff of blue smoke.

Chris was a bit shaken by the experience, but since no one else seemed to be up yet, she continued her walk across the mountain a ways and circled around to approach the camp from the west.

She found the woods of Oz not very different from her own in the Puget Sound Country, except that these had much less in the way of underbrush. There was pine and fir, giant cedar and, at this time of year barren trees that appeared to be vine maple and alder. What there was of undergrowth seemed equally familiar – Oregon grape, blackberry, huckleberry and lots of old dead bracken.

By the time she finally rejoined the others, everyone was up and Ozma was just preparing to put breakfast upon the table. Not wanting to interrupt the process, she waited until the job was done by a few swipes of Ozma's wand. As everyone was being seated, Chris spoke quietly to Ozma, saying "I just met Lorabie. She calls herself a witch, and she was pretty threatening, and confusing, saying she was going to make the

Viridian Mountain

abomination in the valley disappear, connecting it with Christmas and getting rid of that fat old man and his cohorts. She meant Santa Claus, didn't she? Can she do that?"

Ozma took Chris gently by the shoulders and said, "Did she seem like a witch to you?"

"Goodness, yes! And she sounded like she meant what she said."

"I have my doubts," said Ozma. "Nonetheless, in this land, we have to assume that she can do magic. She could cause a lot of trouble. We had better be going quickly."

When the others were told, there was some consternation and the Cowardly Lion worried, "Oh, what are we going to do? This is just too terrifying!"

Everyone ate quickly, checked their tents to be sure nothing had been left behind, and, with a wave of Ozma's wand dishes, tables, chairs and tents were gone. Then off they went, at a rapid walk, on the last leg of their journey.

Chapter 8
A Celebration in the Snow

t still took several hours to reach the summit of Viridian Mountain. There they found the graffittied rock, the snow covered mountains and valley, and the mysterious village. Without pause, Ozma started to lead them directly toward the village when the Cowardly Lion quavered, "Oh-h-h, I am not at all certain this is a good idea."

"Don't worry, friend Lion," spoke up the Hungry Tiger, "There are plenty of us, and you can rip and tear, and so can I and Ozma has her wand. What is there for us to fear?"

"Oh-ah. N-n-noth-th-thing," replied the Lion, as he stationed himself at the front of the line, shoulder to shoulder with the Tiger, "I just am afraid." The others fell

A Celebration in the Snow

in behind them and so the column advanced into the valley.

Suddenly, a great shiver shook the frame of the Cowardly Lion as he whispered loudly, "There's someone here."

"Of course there is," replied Trot. "Quite a crowd of us."

"N-n-no. I mean someone I c-can't see. S-s-someone c-coming towards us and l-leaving footprints without any f-f-feet."

By this time everyone could see that he was speaking the truth. As Ozma stepped forward, starting to wave her wand, there was a laugh and a little man materialized in front of them, saying, "I didn't mean to scare you. I was just supposed to surprise you."

"Peter! What are you doing here?" shouted Trot.

"Is Santa around, too?" asked Dorothy.

"Do you know anything about these buildings?" chimed in Button-Bright.

"Wait. Wait. All in due time," replied the little man. "I just came out to welcome you officially to Christmas Valley. Now we will go on into the village where all your questions will be answered. Come. Follow me," and off he went, toward the village at a rapid pace.

"Well," purred the Lion, "I guess if Peter is involved in it, the village must be safe."

"What did he call it?" asked Button-Bright. "Christmas Valley?"

Christmas in Oz

"I think that's right," answered Trot. "I guess we'll find out all about it as soon as we get there."

Chris pulled gently on Dorothy's sleeve, and whispered, "What was that? Did you say something about Santa, like Santa Claus?"

"Yes," she answered. "He visits us occasionally in the Emerald City, but I've never known him to be way out here."

"Agh. I'll never get use to this. Santa Claus is just a legend! None of this is supposed to be real. But here I am. And it's too real for dreaming. I'll just tramp through this snow that isn't even wet or cold and go along with the rest of you! How will I ever tell anyone what I've been doing? Agggh!" And she laughed and threw one arm around Dorothy and the other around Trot.

In a few minutes more, they were in the village and approaching the large, central inn. As with the others, when they reached the door, they were met by Santa Claus himself.

"Ah ho, fair Queen Ozma and all my good friends, I bid you welcome," he called out cheerily.

"Neclaus," responded Ozma as she ran to him, addressing him as the fairies do, "How good to see you again!"

Holding her in one arm, he reached the other out, saying, "I see you've brought Chris along with you." Then, speaking directly to the newcomer, said, "I was planning to take your gifts to Philadelphia this year, but

66

should I bring them to the Emerald City instead?"

Chris just looked at him, gasped, and opened her mouth, but nothing came out.

"Ho, ho, ho. Cat's got your tongue, hunh? Well that's OK. It probably is a little confusing. But, yes, I am real, and you really are talking to me."

With that, Chris suddenly found her voice, and said, "I'm pleased to meet you, sir, and I'm sorry I didn't believe in you before, but I sure will from now on. Maybe I should even tell the other kids. And no, don't deliver my presents to the Emerald City, because I promised my folks I'd be back with them in Philadelphia before Christmas. And I'm sorry I'm talking so much."

With a deep chuckle, Santa said, "That's OK. When you were too tense to talk, I used a little relaxing magic on you, and I must have overdone it a bit." And both of them laughed some more as Santa Claus continued greeting the rest as they came through the door.

After the last one had been greeted Ozma held Santa back and said, "Neclaus, there's a new development. Chris met an old Munchkin woman, Lorabie, this morning, who styles herself the 'Blue Witch of the East.' Do you know anything about her?"

"The only Munchkin Lorabie I know is certainly no witch, blue or otherwise."

"Well, she told Chris that she is going to get rid of you and all this, make you disappear."

"Humph. I would tend to discount that. But, we had

A Celebration in the Snow

better be on the lookout, nonetheless. As you discovered, my elves are being invisible sentries out there. They will let us know if she comes anywhere near us."

They moved on into the building, where everyone was talking with hardly subdued excitement. Before long, Cap'n Bill moved over toward Ozma. A broad grin broke through the rim of whiskers around his chin, as he said, "Bust my timbers if ya didn't know about this little village all the time. Ha?"

"Exactly so, Cap'n. Santa needed a workshop in Oz, and I was glad to help. He said he would be ready to give us a big surprise party four days before Christmas. And here we are!"

"You mean you were planning on bringing us here anyway, even before this business about the curse came up?" asked Dorothy.

"That's right. Lorabie just gave me an excuse to bring all of you here without telling you the real reason."

Everyone had quieted down to hear this conversation, once it got started, and now they all broke into laughter. So we will leave them to their merriment while we take note of a large, lone apple tree on the south slope of Scarlet Mountain.

As we look, suddenly, the Wizard and Tik-Tok appear nearby.

"Ah, right on the spot," said the Wizard, swinging his black bag of magical instruments and potions in the direction of the tree, "right by this beautiful apple tree."

Christmas in Oz

"Your ma-gic ne-ver fa-ils," answered the mechanical man as they walked toward the tree.

Reaching for the closest of the red fruit, the Wizard commented, "Ah, I wish you could enjoy one of these delicious apples, Tik-Tok."

Then just as his hand touched it, the tree began to shake violently, and a cascade of apples fell upon him and his mechanical friend, knocking them both, rolling across the grass.

Two dark shapes jumped from the tree, Lorabie and Midnight. The Witch quickly grabbed the fallen little black bag, and vaulting onto the leopard's back, she

A Celebration in the Snow

laughed, "Ha, Wizard indeed! Know that I, Lorabie, the Wicked Blue Witch of the East, has just bested you at your own game!" And off she raced on her great cat, over the hills to the east.

"What was that?" clicked Tik-Tok.

"That must have been a new Wicked Witch," answered the Wizard, "the Lorabie who wrote the warnings in the passes. If she knows anything about magic, she can do a lot of harm with that bag!"

"Then we had bet-ter hur-ry to jo-in up with Oz-ma," declared the mechanical man.

"Yes," replied the Wizard, getting up and brushing the leaves from himself. Then, picking up one apple to chew as they rushed off, he added "Guess I'd better forget about any more apples for now."

Soon they were at the pass where the elves quickly ushered them down into Christmas Valley and into Santa's office where they found him and Ozma conferring. After brief greetings, the Wizard informed them of the loss of his Black Bag.

"What next?" asked Santa. "She seems to be popping up all over the place."

"She appears to have done some pretty good magic," said Ozma. "She could be quite a threat."

"Nonetheless, the three of us should well be a match for her," said Santa. They continued talking a while longer, but were soon ready to join the others for lunch.

Everyone enjoyed their meal and the rest of the day

Christmas in Oz

with little thought of the Wicked Witch. This was an opportunity to find out all about Christmas Valley. There were guided tours of everything, or people were free to explore to their heart's content, getting acquainted with Santa's helpers and his reindeer, and watching the various shops at work.

Gradually, people began to move to the outside and began playing in the snow.

Chris was the first to roll some big lumps of snow into a snowman. Before she had finished, others had joined her. One of them altered his to have a beard and smile like Santa's. Cap'n Bill rolled a huge ball onto two snow covered stumps, and with a smaller one on top, made it look like Tik-Tok. By this time Dorothy had made a little one that looked like Toto and Ozma had made one that looked like the Wooden Sawhorse. Before long there was a snowman duplicate of everyone that was there.

The afternoon was getting late, but before they could stop for supper, Scraps had tossed a snowball at Dorothy. She missed and hit Chris. Laughing, both human girls returned a volley of snowballs at the stuffed girl, with a few hitting Uncle Henry and Cap'n Bill. As they returned a fresh fusillade of snow, the girls moved away from the fancy snowmen so they would not be damaged. Others joined them, and soon snow forts were erected and everyone was occupied in a big battle royal.

A Celebration in the Snow

When the dinner bell rang, everyone was ready and devoured their dinners rapidly.

The next day everyone was up early in Christmas Valley. Although quickly finished, breakfast was plenteous. As final mouthfuls were being consumed, Santa Claus stood up to address the gathering. "Ho, ho! Welcome one and all to the grand opening of Christmas Valley. We have games planned in the snow, logs ablaze in the fire, and food a-cooking on the stoves." Then, holding a mug of eggnog aloft, he called out in a cheery voice, "I declare today a holiday! A holiday for all, mortals and immortals alike. No more work shall be done until tomorrow. Today is for decorating and games and celebration of our new workshop! A toast to holiday!"

Everyone had already been brought a mug of eggnog like Santa's, which each now raised high, calling out, "A toast! A toast!" Then all drank heartily of the thick and spicy liquid. As they were finishing, Santa said, "Those who wish can start the day with some final decorating of trees, both inside and out. Those who would rather can just watch or do whatever they wish, and here is Peter with the list of decorating opportunities, so I will turn things over to him."

At first many were not much interested in decorating, but the ones who started doing it were having so much fun that soon, everyone was involved. Time seemed to stand still during those hours and yet, before anyone was ready, the morning was over and the bell rang, calling them to their noontime meal.

Entering the dining hall, they found that each place was set with a steaming bowl of an unfamiliar soup. It had a faint pine-like flavor and floating in each bowl were several miniature green Christmas wreaths composed of some nutty flavored paste. When the main course was brought in, there was roast turkey, roast duck and roast goose. There were white potatoes, sweet potatoes and dressing. There were cranberries and peas and broccoli and beans. Salads of all kinds abounded. Pitchers of both red punch and green punch were passed up and down the tables. Finally, while all the dishes were being cleared away by one group of elves, another group brought in great bowls of flaming plum pudding.

It was a dinner fully fit for even the greatest and most royal of those gathered at the tables. Chris looked around and wondered to herself how she could possibly be in such a situation. Astounding! Just then Santa spoke to her saying, "You know, you are the girl whose name brings me special cheer."

Blushing a bit, she asked, "What do you mean by that?"

"Just think, every time someone calls you be your full name they remind their friends of my special time of year. Did you ever think of that?"

Chris blushed even redder and stammered a bit before she could speak, "I don't quite know how to say

A Celebration in the Snow

this, but the truth is, I've always been kind of embarrassed by my real name because the kids teased me about it so much. That's why I just go by 'Chris.' I'm sorry."

"Now, now. You don't have to be sorry," replied the old gentleman. "Lots of people don't use their real name. Look at the Wizard here."

"I never thought of that," and turning to the little man in black, added, "Of course, 'Wizard' isn't your real name, is it?"

"No," he laughed. "My real name is Oscar Zoroaster Phadrig Isaac Norman Henkle Emmanuel Ambroise Diggs."

"Golly!" she responded, "You've got even a longer name than Button-Bright."

"Yes. And did you notice what my initials spell?"

Chris blushed a little again, as she nodded her head, trying to keep from breaking out into laughter.

"No one wants to go through life being called 'Pinhead', so all I ever used was my first two initials. And that served me in good stead when I came here. But enough about my name: I think you ought to be proud of yours."

"Christmas?" she tried it quizzically. "How would that sound to me for a change?"

Dorothy, sitting next to her, poked her lightly and said, "Well, Christmas, I don't know what you think, but I like it. OK?"

Christmas in Oz

"OK," answered Christmas. "I'm game."

Just as Dorothy was saying, "I'll tell the others," Ozma came over to whisper something in Santa's ear, who then stood up and said, "Who wants to play in the snow?"

His question was met with an immediate chorus of "I do!" "Whoopee!" "Let's go!" and bedlam broke loose as everyone jumped up and headed for the doors. By the time they had all gotten out into the snow, Santa's helpers were bringing sleds, skis and toboggans for all of them.

Again, people remarked on how the snow was neither cold nor wet, and yet everything that could be done with regular snow could be done with this. At first Tik-Tok held back from playing in the snow for fear of what its usual dampness would do to his joints. But, eventually, even he was convinced that there was no wetness at all in Santa's magic snow, and joined the others in speeding down the hills on waxed wood and steel runners. This occupied everyone for several hours until some began leaving the hillside to join in snow games like fox and geese and snow angels.

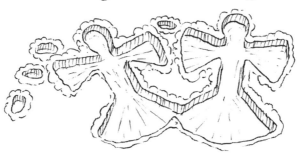

Chapter 9
Lorabie's Curse

histledown, sitting as an invisible sentinel up on Scarlet Mountain, heard someone approaching. Looking toward the sound, he saw a large black leopard coming up the hill with a dark blue-garbed lady astride him. Midnight and Lorabie had finally arrived. Immediately, the elf streaked through the air to tell Santa.

The Blue Witch was carrying the Wizard's little black bag. She had worked late the night before and again all morning trying to figure out how to use his equipment. Actually, now she knew no more than she did when she started, but she thought she did. She began by taking a long hollow tube out and looking through it toward the people at play. She turned it and twisted it and slid the parts back and forth, but she still didn't see anything through it, so she set it aside rather angrily. Next she scattered the contents of several of his packets upon the snow and began dancing around, chanting:

"This will never be.
Cursed may it be.

From thence the curse shall flow
Until it all is done.
Your ending you shall know
For each shall now become
A statue made of snow.

And all because of me.
So says Lorabie!"

Her dance ended in a few more flourishes and some wild stamping in the snow. Then she quickly bent over the little Black Bag, bringing out an instrument which, when she pulled on the handle, made bright sparks. She showered these over the scene of her dance and the potions she had sprinkled around. As some of them caught fire, she cried to Midnight, "Ha. See the curse begins to take effect!" Then jumping upon her back, she added, "Come, we shall go down to see what marvelous statues I have created."

Lorabie's Curse

Soon after those celebrating in the snow had moved away from their snow statues to play other games, Lorabie came creeping around the edge of the village and discovered the hillside of statues. She stopped for a moment, then went over and touched the nearest one, the likeness of Chris. Standing quietly, she finally said, "Such a sweet little girl. Maybe I shouldn't have done this." Then looking beyond he girl, she saw the icy form of Santa Claus, and mused, "I thought I would rejoice in victory to see him all frozen solid like that. But I'm not. I don't feel so good."

Then behind her she heard the voice of Santa Claus, "Not over there, Lorabie. Over here."

She turned to the voice, saw the real Santa Claus as he materialized from his invisible state, and said, "How can there be two of you? I cast the charm myself, making you a snow statue!"

"I know," he responded, "but I guess it didn't work, did it?"

Appearing beside him, Ozma added, "We've been studying Santa's lists and we know what a hard life you've had: the teasing when you were young, then all those years in an isolated cabin way up in the mountains, no family, no neighbors, no friends until you rescued Midnight a few years ago. Then when you moved down to the settled land last year, you were awkward, being around people as you had not been since childhood, and they called you a 'witch.'"

Christmas in Oz

"So," continued Santa, "you decided to try to be what they said you were."

"But you don't have to be a witch," Ozma reassured her. "You can just be a nice friendly lady with your big cat."

Lorabie looked at the two of them. Tears began to form in her eyes, but she fought them back.

Santa said, "That's okay, my dear. We love you just as you are."

"Yes," continued Ozma, "we know all about what you tried to do, but that doesn't matter. We can love you in any case."

"It doesn't matter," said Santa, "that you drilled holes in the road to stop the Sawhorse. He was repaired all right. Since it looked like rain, you pretended to cause it. You did some slight-of-hand tricks and of course your attempt to turn us all into snow statues didn't work. These are just snowmen that everybody made for the fun of it. But all that doesn't matter between friends."

"We love you anyway," said Ozma.

Now Lorabie really was crying and wailing through her big blue handkerchief, "Oh, it's so unfair! Why can't anything ever work out for me?"

Ozma took her in her arms, saying, "That's all right. You've been many a year without tears. But everything's all right now. You are among friends." She continued to hold Lorabie and comfort her.

As the tears began to subside, Santa Claus said, "Tell

us about Ehrven."

Lorabie's face went ashen. She choked and sobbed some more. Finally she stammered, "H-how d-did you know? I've never told anyone. I've tried to forget."

"Maybe it would be good to talk about it now," continued the old gentleman.

"He was so good, so handsome. It was many years ago. I was young and so was he. Born in the same year, we had grown up next door to each other. All through our childhood we did everything together. We learned to dance hand in hand. We were always a pair. The first time we didn't do something together was when I decided to stop aging at sixteen and he went on to twenty.

"Early in those four years, I discovered that I was in love with him – madly in love. He could do almost anything. He was all I could ever want. I loved him so I was certain that he loved me. After all, we always did everything together.

"But then I would see him out with other girls and holding hands and I would fly into a frenzy. He couldn't understand what upset me so. One morning he rushed into my home saying, 'I've got the most wonderful news!'

"I thought, *Maybe he's finally come to his senses and realizes that he is in love with me.* But no! He wanted to tell . . . to let me be the first to know that he and Mattille had decided to get married!

Christmas in Oz

"I went crazy, striking at him, calling him all kinds of names and chasing him out of the house.

"But a few days later I went to see him again. I asked him why did he love Mattille and not me. Was she prettier than I? More clever? What did he see in her?

"'Lorabie, you are the best friend I've ever had,' he told me, 'but I've never had any romantic feelings for you. Sure, you're pretty and smart and lots of fun. But we've been friends for ever so long and I could never think of you in any other way. I always want us to be best friends.'

"I stuck around until the marriage, hoping he'd come back to me, but he never did. He went right ahead and married Mattille. And that was that. I left my home, never to return. I moved far away from everybody and allowed myself to grow old."

All the time Lorabie was talking, she was also crying tears by the bucketful. Now she smiled through the tears, "That's the first time I've ever talked about this to anyone, not even to Midnight. And you know what? I do feel better."

"I'm glad," said Ozma, holding the weeping old lady close. "We know all about your story. Santa's records are very complete. We know how you have lived alone for one hundred and twenty years, hating everyone because you could not have the one you loved. Then five years ago, Midnight showed up on your doorstep in the middle of the night—just a wee little, whimpering cub.

Lorabie's Curse

Your heart, empty of all caring for so long, went out to her."

Santa Claus picked it up at this point, saying, "Then when you came down to where other people lived last year, people saw you with Midnight and mistook you for a witch. And that's when you began to plot your revenge on the whole world."

"But you don't have to be a witch," said Ozma. "You can just be a nice friendly lady with your own big cat."

"And now," said Santa, "it's time for supper. So come and join us."

Just then, the three girls came over the hill. They were covered with snow, their hair in disarray, but when Christmas saw Lorabie, she called out, "Oh, there she is. Miss Lorabie, show them your trick with the coin. They don't believe me when I tell them that you can make it disappear."

A bit flustered, Lorabie looked at Santa and Ozma, both smiling at her, then at the eager young girls running up to her. And she made a decision. She smiled at them, pulled a coin from a pocket and went through the same routine she had with Chris, but this time, after showing her empty hands, she reached behind Dorothy's ear and pulled a coin out which she flipped high into the air. Before it landed in her outstretched left hand, she had reached into the hair on top of Trot's head and pulled out another, which she also flipped into the air. Then another from Santa's beard, a fourth

Christmas in Oz

from one of Ozma's poppies, and a fifth appeared to come right out of Christmas's mouth. When that last one clicked into her left hand, she showed the coins and then closed her fist again, waved her right hand over it while she recited, "Muzzle beu, fizzle fop," and showed both hands, now empty once again.

The girls crowded around, eagerly begging her to do it attain, but she only smiled and waggled her finger back and forth, saying, "Only once. Only once!" Then she turned and took the lead, back toward the buildings.

On the way, Ozma whispered to Christmas, "I'm glad

Lorabie's Curse

you asked Lorabie to show the other girls that coin trick. It was just what she needed to assure her that she really is welcome here."

Before she had finished speaking, Skydew struck a silver triangle and called out, "Soup's on!" bringing everyone, trooping in through the various doors of the dining hall. Bowls of delicious barley soup awaited them, along with their choice of red or green eggnog. Most took one of each color. After supper Santa Claus brought out ice skates in all shapes and sizes to fit every person and creature there. There was even a special little round set to fit the four hooves of the sawhorse and huge ones for the feet of the Cowardly Lion, the Hungry Tiger and Midnight.

It was dark now with no moon, but Santa had magic to make it as bright outside as though there were a big full moon. Throughout the evening the happy voices of the skaters could be heard. Bonfires were lit with pots of cocoa warming on them, and whenever anyone wanted to rest, he or she could find others ready to chat at one of the fires. Although the snow itself was not cold, the night air in this high altitude had a distinct chill to it, and the warmth of the fire without and the cocoa within was always welcome.

One of the earliest groups around the fires included Ozma, the Wizard and Lorabie. The former witch was saying, "You have all been so kind to me, and after the way I tried to hurt all of you, I feel very ashamed of myself."

"Don't feel ashamed," replied Ozma. "Just be happy that you have found friends at last."

"Yes," said the Wizard, "and remember, you have learned something that many people never do – being pleasant is easier and lots more fun than getting even and being mean."

"I'd certainly be glad to tell them," answered the ex-witch. "And by the way, I don't think I really want to go around dressed as a witch any more. I'm going to make myself some new clothes when I get home!"

"Why wait?" asked Ozma as she touched her Magic Belt and mumbled a few words. Suddenly, Lorabie's witch's outfit lost its mystic symbols and became an ordinary blue Munchkin outfit. "Now, if that's not what you want, I can turn it right back or make some more changes. What do you think?"

Instead of saying anything, Lorabie just started crying, not hard, but nonetheless real. Finally her words were, "Oh, Ozma, I don't know how I can ever thank you."

"You will never have to do that. As ruler of Oz, it is my pleasure to help my subjects in any way I can. So let's just go skate."

And they did.

Hours later, after he completed a magnificent figure eight on the ice, Santa called out, "Ho, now. It is nearing midnight. Ho, ho, ho! We must bring this day of festivity

Lorabie's Curse

to an end."

"Just a little longer, please," cried a sleepy Button-Bright.

"Now, now," said Dorothy, taking him by the hand. "Come on. I'll help you get your skates off."

Soon everyone was back in the main chalet, going to whatever room Peter had assigned to each of them. It had been a day of great fun and excitement. And for that very reason it had also been a long and tiring day. Everyone who could feel anything felt warm and comfortable, and weary too. So everyone man, woman, child and beast was well ready for a good night's sleep.

CHAPTER 10

Return Home

he next morning, everyone was busy getting ready for the trip back to the Emerald City. Lorabie and Midnight had been invited to travel with them and to spend the Christmas holiday at the Palace. It was an uneventful trip and by time for dinner on the second day, they were back in the palace.

After dinner was all over, Chris said "Goodbye" to all her new friends and gave Lorabie a hug and a kiss on the cheek. Then Ozma, using her Magic Belt, sent both Christmas and the umbrella back to her uncle's in Philadelphia. Watching in the Magic Picture, Ozma, Dorothy and Trot saw Christmas run into her mother's arms, give her a hug and a kiss and then to her father and to Uncle Walt and Aunt Lydia.

Return Home

Watching them, Ozma let the picture fade as Christmas began to tell them of her wonderful adventures in Oz. And my, you can guess what excitement that caused in the von Smith house, how she actually met Dorothy, Ozma, the Cowardly Lion, the Wizard and Santa Claus! And all about the wicked witch. And finding Uncle Walt's long lost older brother, Saladin, who was still only about nine years old! Oh, what an evening that was!

The next morning, Christmas morning, was practically an anticlimax. But there were those five unexplained packages under the tree. They were wrapped in green with yellow ribbon, and no one knew where they had come from. Chris had her suspicions, so she insisted that she go last. And she was not surprised when the adults all got emerald jewelry – dangling earrings for her mother, a lovely brooch for Aunt Lydia, a tie tack for her father and an emerald studded belt for Uncle Walt.

Then all looked to see what was in the package for Chris. It was larger than the others, and she opened it with cautious eagerness. She undid the ribbon, folded back the paper and there sat a beautiful brand new Oz book – *Christmas in Oz*.

"Oh," she cried out, "There really is a Santa Claus."

The End

The Oz Books

If you have enjoyed this book, you might be interested in the International Wizard of Oz Club. Not only does it publish *The Baum Bugle* three times a year, a magazine with much valuable information and opinion about Oz and things related to it, but it also arranges for regional meetings of people interested in Oz and tells you about other Oz events going on in the world. Contact:

The International Wizard of Oz Club
P. O. Box 2657
Alameda CA, 94501, USA
or
www.ozcub.org

What is an Oz book? A very few people declare that only *The Wizard of Oz* is eligible. A few more limit them to the books by L. Frank Baum. Most people accept the Famous Forty, that is, *The Wizard of Oz* plus the 39 Oz books published by Reilly & Britton and its successor, Reilly and Lee. Many, including this author, add to that the other fairy tales of Baum whose characters or places he brought into the Oz books (known as the Borderland of Oz Books) and any other Oz book written by the authors of the Famous Forty as well as any published by the International Wizard of Oz Club by such authors as Dick Martin and Virginia Wickwar. This author would add to those any other Oz books written in the spirit of the Baum-Thompson books. Of course that

Christmas in Oz

is a highly subjective standard of judgment, but in the following list, that means the seven Shanower books, and some by Gjovaag-Carlson, Hess and Eichorn. Other people would include any book that has the word Oz in the title, extending the list to hundreds.

Most Oz books are available from Books of Wonder, 16 W. 18th Street, New York, NY 10011, www.booksofwonder.com; or amazon.com, used and sometimes new. Several, as noted, are more easily available from Hungry Tiger Press [HTP], 5995 Dandridge Lane, Suite 121, San Diego CA 92115, www.hungrytigerpress.com; or International Wizard of Oz Club [IWOC], P.O. Box 26249, San Francisco CA 9426-6249, www.ozclub.org.

By L. Frank Baum
1. *The Wizard of Oz*
2. *The Magical Monarch of Mo*
3. *Dot and Tot of Merryland*
4. *The Life and Adventures of Santa Claus*
5. *The Enchanted Island of Yew*
6. *The Land of Oz*
7. *Queen Zixi of Oz*
8. *John Dough and the Cherub*
9. *Ozma of Oz*
10. *Dorothy and the Wizard of Oz*
11. *The Road to Oz*
12. *The Emerald City of Oz*
13. *Sea Fairies*
14. *Sky Island*
15. *The Patchwork Girl of Oz*
16. *Tik-Tok of Oz*
17. *The Scarecrow of Oz*
18. *Rinkitink in Oz*
19. *The Lost Princess of Oz*
20. *The Tin Woodman of Oz*
21. *The Magic of Oz*
22. *Glinda of Oz*

The Oz Books

By Ruth Plumly Thompson
23. *The Royal Book of Oz*
24. *Kabumpo in Oz*
25. *The Cowardly Lion of Oz*
26. *Grampa in Oz*
27. *The Lost King of Oz*
28. *The Hungry Tiger of Oz*
29. *The Gnome King of Oz*
30. *The Giant Horse of Oz*
31. *Jack Pumpkinhead of Oz*
32. *The Yellow Knight of Oz*
33. *Pirates in Oz*
34. *The Purple Prince of Oz*
35. *Ojo in Oz*
36. *Speedy in Oz*
37. *The Wishing Horse of Oz*
38. *Captain Salt in Oz*
39. *Handy Mandy in Oz*
40. *The Silver Princess in Oz*
41. *Ozoplaning with the Wizard in Oz*

By John R. Neill
42. *The Wonder City of Oz*
43. *The Scalawagons of Oz*
44. *Lucky Bucky in Oz*

By Jack Snow
45. *The Magical Mimics in Oz*
46. *The Shaggy Man of Oz*

By Rachel Cosgrove Payes
47. *The Hidden Valley of Oz*

By Eloise Jarvis McGraw &
    Lauren McGraw Wagner
48. *Merry Go Round in Oz*

By Ruth Plumly Thompson
49. *Yankee in Oz*
50. *The Enchanted Island of Oz*

By Eloise Jarvis McGraw &
    Lauren McGraw Wagner
51. *The Forbidden Fountain of Oz*

By Dick Martin
52. The Ozmapolitan of Oz

By Eric Shanower (graphic novels)
53. *The Enchanted Apples of Oz* [HTP]
54. *The Secret Island of Oz* [HTP]
55. *The Ice King of Oz* [HTP]
56. *The Forgotten Forest of Oz* [HTP]
57. *The Blue Witch of Oz* [HTP]

By Rachel Gosgrove Payes
58. *The Wicked Witch of Oz* [IWOC]

93

Christmas in Oz

Who's Who

Aunt Em – Dorothy's Aunt. From *The Wizard of Oz.* 2, 19, 33-53, 71-88.

Aunt Lydia – Chris's Aunt in Philadelphia. 9-10, 18-9, 88-9.

Bill Weedles – See *Cap'n Bill Weedles.*

Billy-Billy Bleep-Bleep – The light green clad elf that specializes in mechanical toys. 44-58, 64-5, 105.

Birdswing – The rose clad elf that specializes in making flying things. 44-58.

Black leopard – See *Midnight.*

Blue Witch – See *Lorabie.*

Bubbles – The light blue clad elf that specializes in making balloons and other stretchy things. 44-58.

Button-Bright – A little boy, originally from Philadelphia, who got lost so often, he finally settled in Oz. From *The Road to Oz.* 4, 6, 8, 15, 22-30, 62-9, 71-88.

Cap'n Bill Weedles – Retired, peg-legged sea captain who came to Oz with Trot. From *Sea Fairies.* 2, 15, 19, 25, 28, 31-53, 71-88.

Caretaker of the Viridian Springs – See *Springer.*

Children – At farmhouse on way to Springer's cottage. 26-7.

Chris – See *Merry Christmas Pederson.*

Cowardly Lion – From *The Wizard of Oz.* 14-6, 22-30, 62-9, 71-88.

Dorothy – Heroine of this and many Oz books. From *The Wizard of Oz.* 1-5, 7, 15-6, 22-30, 62-9, 71-88.

Dragon – Referred to by Birdswing. 56.

Christmas in Oz

Ehrven – The young man that Lorabie grew up with and fell in love with, but he married another. [*Ehr* sounds like "air," *ven* rhymes with "when;" *Her'ven*] 81-2.

Elves – Santa's traditional helpers at the North Pole are also present in Christmas Valley. See especially *Billy-Billy Bleep-Bleep*, *Birdswing*, *Bubbles*, *Riddles*, *Skydew* and *Thistledown*.

Father Pedersen – Chris's father. 9-10, 16-9, 88-9.

Glinda – Ruler of the Quadlings in the south of Oz and the most powerful worker of magic in Oz. Both a Good Witch and a Sorceress. 35.

Great-great-and-ever-so-great-grandfather - Distant ancestor of the von Smiths. 9.

Hungry Tiger – From *Ozma of Oz*. 14-6, 22-30, 62-9, 71-88.

Knooks – Santa's helpers with special responsibility for animals. 54-5.

Lorabie – The Wicked Blue Witch of the East, although she turns out not to have any witching powers and in the end, she reforms. [*Lor* like "lore," *a* as in "another," *bie* like "bee;" *Lor'a-bie*] 5-6, 31-9, 42, 60-2, 68-72, 77-88.

Mattille – The woman that Ehrven married. [*a* as in "another," *i* as in "machine"; *mat'ti-lle*] 81-2.

Merrie Christmas Pedersen – The young lady from Olympia, who, visiting her Uncle Walt and Aunt Lydia in Philadelphia, makes use of the Magic Umbrella. 7-30, 59-69, 71-89.

Midnight – Lorabie's familiar, a black leopard. 32, 37-8,

Who's Who

60-2, 70-1, 77-88.

Mother – At farmhouse on way to Springer's cottage. 26-7.

Mother Pedersen – Chris's mother. 8-10, 16-9, 88.

Neclaus – the name Santa Claus is known by among the fairies and their friends. 66, 68, 74, 76.

Nome King – One of the well-known characters in the Oz books. 7.

Nymphs – See *Wood Nymphs*.

Omby Amby – See *Soldier with the Green Whiskers*.

Ozma – The ruler of Oz, a Princess and a Queen. From *The Land of Oz*. 2-7, 14-30, 33, 52, 62, 71-89.

Quadlings – People who live in the southern part of Oz, the Quadling Country. 52.

Patchwork Girl – A life-size, living doll made of a patchwork quilt. From *The Patchwork Girl of Oz*. 19, 32-53, 71-88.

Peter – Although his description is based on Black Peter of Dutch mythology, he was a knook in *The Life and Adventures of Santa Claus*, and is Santa's chief helper. 44-8, 65-6, 73, 85.

Reindeer – 59, 61-3, 80, 72.

Riddles – The brown clad elf that specializes in making puzzles and tricks. 44-58.

Ryls – Santa's helpers who care for flowers and other plants. 54-5.

Saladin – A famous Muslim warrior during the Crusades. 24.

Christmas in Oz

Saladin Paracelsus de Lambertine Evagne von Smith –
See *Button-Bright.*

Santa Claus – 45, 48-54, 65-9, 71-88.

Sawhorse – See *Wooden Sawhorse.*

Scraps – See *Patchwork Girl.*

Skydew – The dark green clad elf that is the cook. 44-58, 85.

Soldier with the Green Whiskers – The Army of Oz, who does sentry duty and in this story is left in charge in the Palace while Ozma and others are investigating Viridian Springs. 6, 14, 22.

Springer – The Caretaker of the Viridian Springs. 2-6, 40, 42.

Thistledown – The light silver-gray clad elf that specializes in stuffing things like pillows, teddy bears and dolls. 44-58, 77.

Tik-Tok – A mechanical man. From *Ozma of Oz.* 7, 14-6, 20-1, 69-88.

Toto – Dorothy's dog. From *The Wizard of Oz.* 2.

Trot – Princess and close friend of Ozma and Dorothy who came to Oz from California. From *Sea Fairies.* 1-4, 6, 15-6, 25-30, 62-9, 71-88.

Uncle Henry – Dorothy's uncle. From *The Wizard of Oz.* 2, 19, 33-53, 71-88.

Uncle Walt – 8-11, 18-9, 25, 28, 88-9.

Von Smith – Family name of Button-Bright, Aunt Lydia and Uncle Walt.

Weedles – See *Cap'n Bill.*

Who's Who

Wicked Blue Witch of the East – See *Lorabie*.

Wizard – The Wizard of Oz, a humbug when first introduced, but after leaving Oz by balloon, a few years later, he returns and is trained to be a real Wizard by Glinda (q. v.). From *The Wizard of Oz*. 20-1, 35, 69-88.

Wood nymphs – Santa's helpers concerned with the care of trees and working with wooden things. 54-5.

Wooden Sawhorse – An old carpenter's sawhorse that Ozma brought to life. From *The Land of Oz*. 19, 32-53.

Where's Where

Arabia – The Middle Eastern country where the von Smith's ancestor obtained the Magic Umbrella. 9.

California – The place that Trot and Cap'n Bill came from. 2.

China – One of the lands that had umbrellas for thousands of years. 10.

Christmas Valley – Chosen as an Ozian center for Santa's work. It is named after my mother's dream of having a holly ranch and collie kennel named Christmas Valley. 3, 5, 40-58, 64-9, 71-88.

East Gate – One of the four principal gates leading into the Emerald City. 19.

Egypt – One of the lands that had umbrellas for thousands of years. 10.

Emerald City – Capital and largest city of Oz. From *The Wizard of Oz.* 4, 12-23, 31, 46, 52, 69, 88-9.

Emerald City area – The area where green predominates surrounding the Emerald City. 23-30, 59-71.

Europe – The area mentioned where umbrellas did not exist until the 17th Century. 10.

Fairy Realms – All the lands where fairies dwell. 52.

Farmhouse –Where the travelers from the Emerald City stopped for lunch. 26.

Hohaho – See *Laughing Valley.*

House – The one belonging to Lorabie. 31-8.

Kansas – Original home of Dorothy, Aunt Em and Uncle Henry. 2.

Laughing Valley of Hohaho – Just outside the forest

of Burzee, this is the location of Santa's original workshop. 45, 52, 53, 60.

Middle East – One of the lands that had umbrellas for thousands of years. 10.

Mo – A country across the Deadly Desert from Oz. 23, 25.

Mortal Lands – All the lands of mortal people on Earth or elsewhere. 51.

Munchkin Country – The blue eastern portion of Oz. 18-9, 31-40.

North Pole – Santa's traditional workshop on Earth. 45, 53.

Olympia, Washington – Home of Chris. 7, 15, 60.

Oz – The magical fairyland in another dimension or parallel universe and locus of the Oz stories. From *The Wizard of Oz*. 1-6, 12-89.

Ozma's apartment – 17-9, 88-9.

Palace – Home of Ozma, Dorothy and many other major characters in Oz. From *The Wizard of Oz*. 1, 4-22, 88-9.

Philadelphia, Pennsylvania – Where Chris is visiting her Uncle Walt and Aunt Lydia. 7-12, 15-6, 18-9, 25, 66, 68, 88-9.

Puget Sound Country – 26, 62.

Quadling Country – The southern part of Oz. 52.

Scarlet Mountain – In the northeast corner of the Quadling. 21, 33, 40, 69-71, 77.

South Gate – One of the four principal gates leading

into the Emerald City. 22.

Springer's cottage – 22, 28-30, 33, 59.

Switzerland – 41.

Viridian Mountain – A mountain in the southeast corner of the Emerald City area. 5, 20, 33, 40, 53, 59-64.

Viridian Springs – A spring on Viridian Mountain that is a major source of water for the Emerald City. 2, 33.

Von Smith home – 7-11, 18-9.

Yellow Brick Road – There is one going form the Emerald City into the Munchkin country at least as far as where Dorothy's house landed on the Wicked Witch of the East. From *The Wizard of Oz*. 19, 31-9.

Alder - Trees found in the Emerald City area as in the Puget Sound Country. 62.

Apple tree – Lorabie and Midnight hid in this tree on the south slope of Scarlet Mountain. 69.

Balloon – 20.

Barley soup – Served as supper at Christmas Valley. 85.

Blackberry – Underbrush found in the Emerald City area as in the Puget Sound Country. 62.

Bracken – Underbrush found in the Emerald City area as in the Puget Sound Country. 62.

Candied orange peel – A special sweet-tart candy that use to be popular at Christmas time. 51.

Cart – One was pulled by the Cowardly Lion and Hungry Tiger on the trip that ended at Christmas Valley. 14, 22.

Cave – 21.

Cedar – Trees found in the Emerald City area as in the Puget Sound Country. 62.

Coins – With which Lorabie does slight-of-hand tricks. 60-1, 83-4.

Crusades – The terrible time when many of the Christians of Europe attacked the Muslims in the Middle East, trying to take Jerusalem away from them. 24.

Eggnog – Available in either red or green in Christmas Valley. 85.

Fir – Trees found in the Emerald City area as in the Puget Sound Country. 62.

Fruit cake – Christmas sweet served at Christmas Valley - 51.

Huckleberry - Underbrush found in the Emerald City area as in the Puget Sound Country. 62.

Ice skates - Adapted in Christmas Valley to fit the feet of everyone and animals too. 85.

Jet airplanes - Some of them fly over the North Pole. 53.

Lorabie's magic paraphernalia - It isn't really magic. 35-7.

Maple - Trees found in the Emerald City area as in the Puget Sound Country. 62.

Marzipan - An almond confection especially prevalent at Christmas time. 51.

Note to parents - 17-9.

Oregon grape - Underbrush found in the Emerald City area as in the Puget Sound Country. 62.

Pine - Trees found in the Emerald City area as in the Puget Sound Country. 62.

Punch - Red or green drink served at Christmas Valley 51.

Red Wagon - A fancy wagon, usually drawn by the Wooden Sawhorse. 19, 32-3.

Rocks with messages - found at all the pases surrounding Christmas Valley. 3, 5, 6 (ill.), 42, 60, 64.

Skis - In use at Christmas Valley. 76.

Sleds - In use at Christmas Valley. 76.

Snickerdoodle - A soft centered Christmas cookie with a crispy exterior popular at Christmas time. 51.

What's What

Snow statues – In the forms of Santa Claus, Tik-Tok, Toto, Wooden Sawhorse, Chris and everyone. 72, 79.

Speculaas – A cakelike almond/ginger cookie, with a Dutch origin and especially popular at Christmas time. 51.

Sugar cookies – Christmas cookies served at Christmas Valley – 51.

Toboggans – In use at Christmas Valley. 76.

Tool box under back seat of Red Wagon – 37.

Well – At Springer's cottage. 59-60.

Magical Magic

(Abbreviations for who has this magic:
Ch = Chris; Om= Ozma; SC = Santa Claus)

Black bag – This little bag contains most of the Wizard's principle magical tools – 69-70, 77.
Changing hair color (Om) – 29.
Magic Belt (Om) – 16, 18, 53, 88.
Magic Picture (Om) – 18, 88-9.
Making table service appear or disappear (Om) – 28-30.
Producing food by magic (Om) – 27-9, 62.
Making tables and chairs appear or disappear (Om) – 28, 63.
Making tent, bedding and night clothes appear or disappear (Om) – 30, 63.
Relaxing magic (SC) – 68.
Umbrella (Ch) – 8-25.

Made in the USA
Charleston, SC
29 December 2012